The Night Before Summer Vacation

Grosset & Dunlap, Publishers

To the Lazutin family—N.W.

To David & Rachel, who are
especially good at vacations—J.D.

Text copyright © 2002 by Natasha Wing. Illustrations copyright © 2002 by Julie Durrell. All rights reserved.
Published by Grosset & Dunlap, a division of Penguin Young Readers Group, 345 Hudson Street, New York,
New York 10014. GROSSET & DUNLAP is a trademark of Penguin Group (USA) Inc. Printed in the U.S.A.

Library of Congress Cataloging-in-Publication Data is available.

ISBN 978-0-448-42830-7   19 20 18

The Night Before Summer Vacation

By Natasha Wing

Illustrated by Julie Durrell

Grosset & Dunlap, Publishers

'Twas the night before leaving
on summer vacation.
My family was bursting
with anticipation.

Dad made a checklist
which he checked as he went—
the bug spray, the backpacks,
the umbrella and tent.

Mom grabbed the graham crackers and stuff for the s'mores.

We carried out helmets,
the canoe, and the oars.
"Remember my raft,
my snorkel, and bike,
plus Pete's doggy bowls,
and Jimmy's new trike."

Down from the attic our suitcases came,
Mom whistled and shouted as if reffing a game:
"In bathing suits! In flip-flops! In sunblock and hats!
In flashlight! In lounge chairs! And Wiffle Ball bats!
To the top of the pile! To the top of the heap!
Now pack away! Pack away! Five layers deep!"

We stuffed and we filled
every inch of the shell.
Like a water balloon,
it started to swell.

Done with our packing,
we ate dinner at last.

Then we got out the scrapbooks
of vacations past.

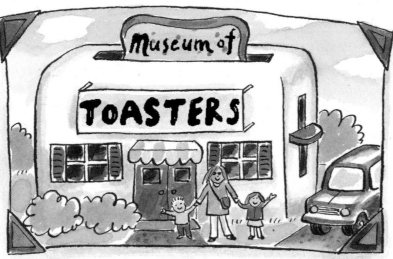

There were photos of us
at the Museum of Toasters.

And my father and I
riding fast roller coasters.

"Here's Jimmy on Babe
and me with Paul Bunyan!"

"And there's Mommy beside
the world's largest onion."

We laughed about trips
we'd taken before.
Our week at the beach
did nothing but pour!

It was so cold
that we all wore our fleeces,
but we finished a puzzle
with two thousand pieces.

At last it was time
to climb into our beds,
where visions of marshmallows
danced in our heads.

In the morning Dad shouted,
"Get up! Rise and shine!
It's quarter to four.
Let's leave here on time!"

Then a few moments later there arose such a clatter,
we ran to the window to see what was the matter.

When what to our wondering eyes should appear,
but Dad, the camper, and a long trail of gear!
He chuckled and said, "Let's hit the road
before our camper decides to explode!"

We all squeezed in,
then drove down our street.

I suddenly cried out,
"Yikes! We forgot Pete!"

Dad made a U-turn,

and Pete jumped inside.

Now we were ready
for the ten-hour ride.

I heard Jimmy ask,
as we drove out of sight,
"Mommy, are we there yet?"
She said, "With luck, by tonight."